D1416505

To Sasha and Liza x

First published in 2020 by Child's Play (International) Ltd
Ashworth Road, Bridgemead, Swindon SN5 7YD, UK

First published in USA in 2020 by Child's Play Inc
250 Minot Avenue, Auburn, Maine 04210

Distributed in Australia by Child's Play Australia Pty Ltd
Unit 10/20 Narabang Way, Belrose, Sydney, NSW 2085

ISBN 978-1-78628-635-2
SJ110621CPL08216352

Printed in Shenzhen, China

1 3 5 7 9 10 8 6 4 2

A catalogue record of this book
is available from the British Library

www.childs-play.com

Best Friends, Busy Friends

Susan Rollings illustrated by Nichola Cowdery

Our friends, best friends,

those who wake us up friends!

Busy friends, helpful friends,

time to go to school friends.

Slow friends,

fast friends,

running around the playground friends.

Tall friends,
GLUE
GLUE
PAPER
small friends,

learning how to read friends.

messy friends,

Tidy friends,

kind and very caring friends.

Singing friends, dancing friends,

hopping, skipping,
jumping friends!

Funny friends, silly friends,

sometimes not so kind friends!

Wet friends,

swimming friends,

splashing in the water friends.

Still friends,

quiet friends,

reading us a story friends.

Sad friends,

happy friends,

skipping home from school friends.

Furry friends,

feathered friends,

lots of very hungry friends!

Our friends, happy friends,

home and after school friends.

Fluffy friends, nosy friends,

off to meet important friends.

Best friends, special friends,

surprise, surprise! It's all our friends!